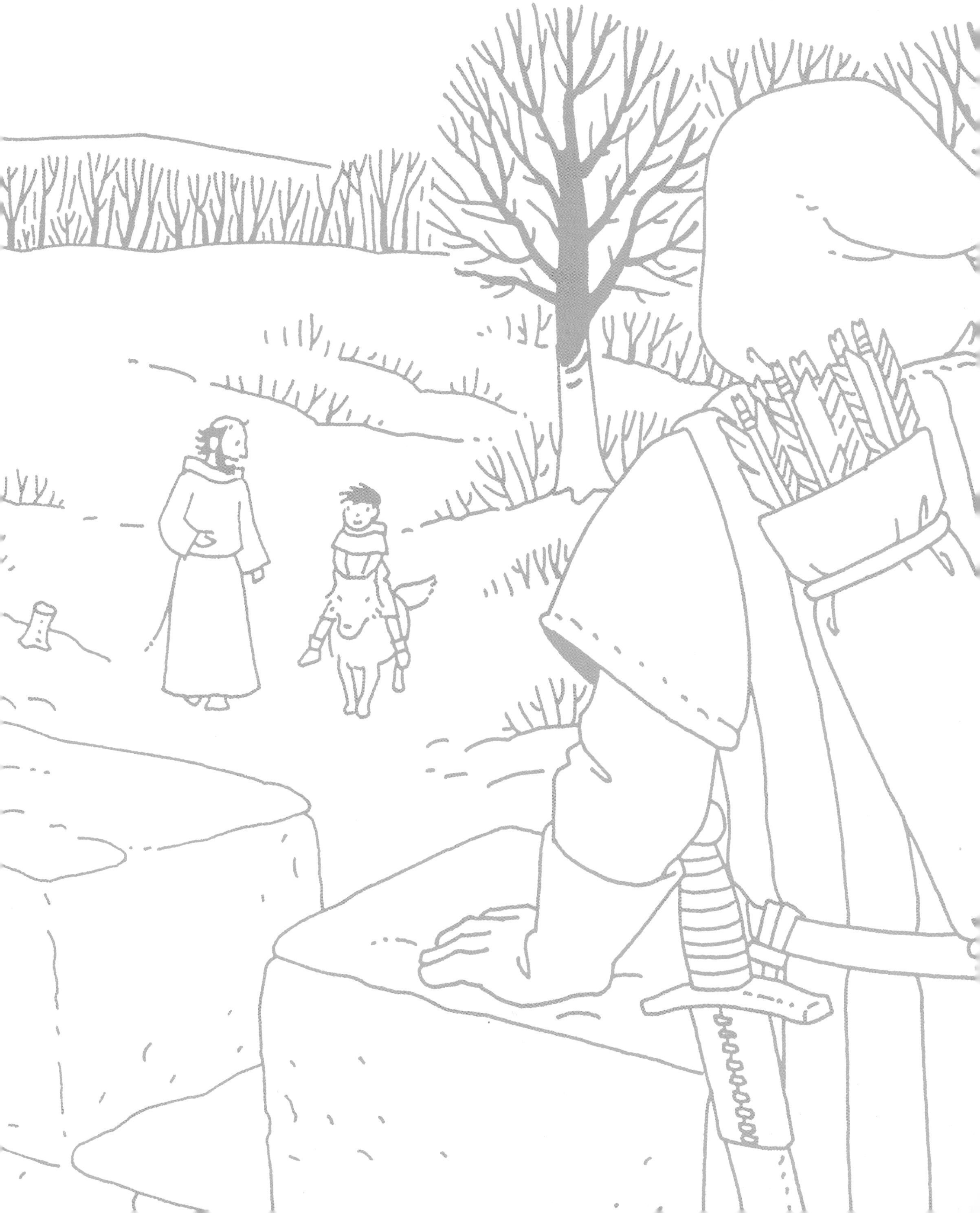

Jean-François Kieffer

The Adventures of LOUPiO

Translated by Janet Chevrier

VOLUME 3

The Tournament

Ignatius

MAGNIFICAT.

Original French edition: *Les Aventures de Loupio*
Tome 4: Le Tournoi
© 2003 by Fleurus-Edifa, Paris
© 2013 by Ignatius Press, San Francisco • Magnificat USA LLC, New York
All rights reserved
ISBN Ignatius Press 978-1-58617-853-6
ISBN Magnificat 978-1-936260-63-8

The trademark MAGNIFICAT depicted in this publication is used under license
from and is the exclusive property of Magnificat Central Service Team, Inc.,
A Ministry to Catholic Women, and may not be used without its written consent.

Printed by Tien Wah Press, Singapore
Printed on July 29, 2013
Job Number MGN 13012
Printed in compliance with the Consumer Protection Safety Act of 2008.

FRANCIS OF ASSISI

lived a poor but joyful life during
the era of knights and troubadours. Son of
a rich merchant of the city of Assisi in Italy,
this young man decided to give up his fortune
and his dreams of glory so as to serve God
better. Free from material goods, he became
a brother and a friend to all living creatures.
It is said that Francis spoke to birds and
that one day he changed a wolf's heart.
Some even say that this wolf befriended
an orphan child and that the two of them
roamed the roads of Italy, having
a thousand adventures …

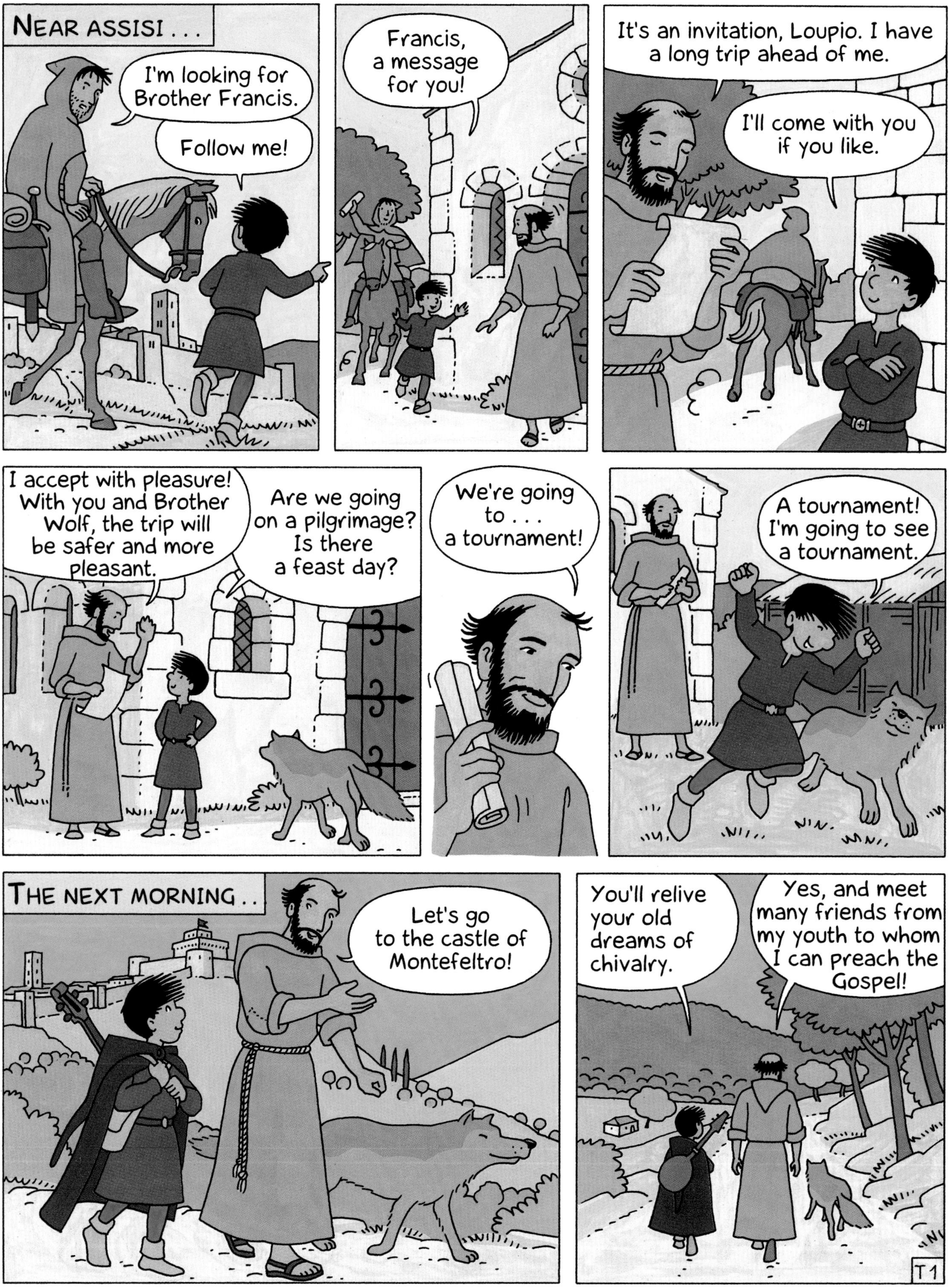

NEAR ASSISI . . .
I'm looking for Brother Francis.
Follow me!
Francis, a message for you!
It's an invitation, Loupio. I have a long trip ahead of me.
I'll come with you if you like.
I accept with pleasure! With you and Brother Wolf, the trip will be safer and more pleasant.
Are we going on a pilgrimage? Is there a feast day?
We're going to . . . a tournament!
A tournament! I'm going to see a tournament.
THE NEXT MORNING . .
Let's go to the castle of Montefeltro!
You'll relive your old dreams of chivalry.
Yes, and meet many friends from my youth to whom I can preach the Gospel!
T1

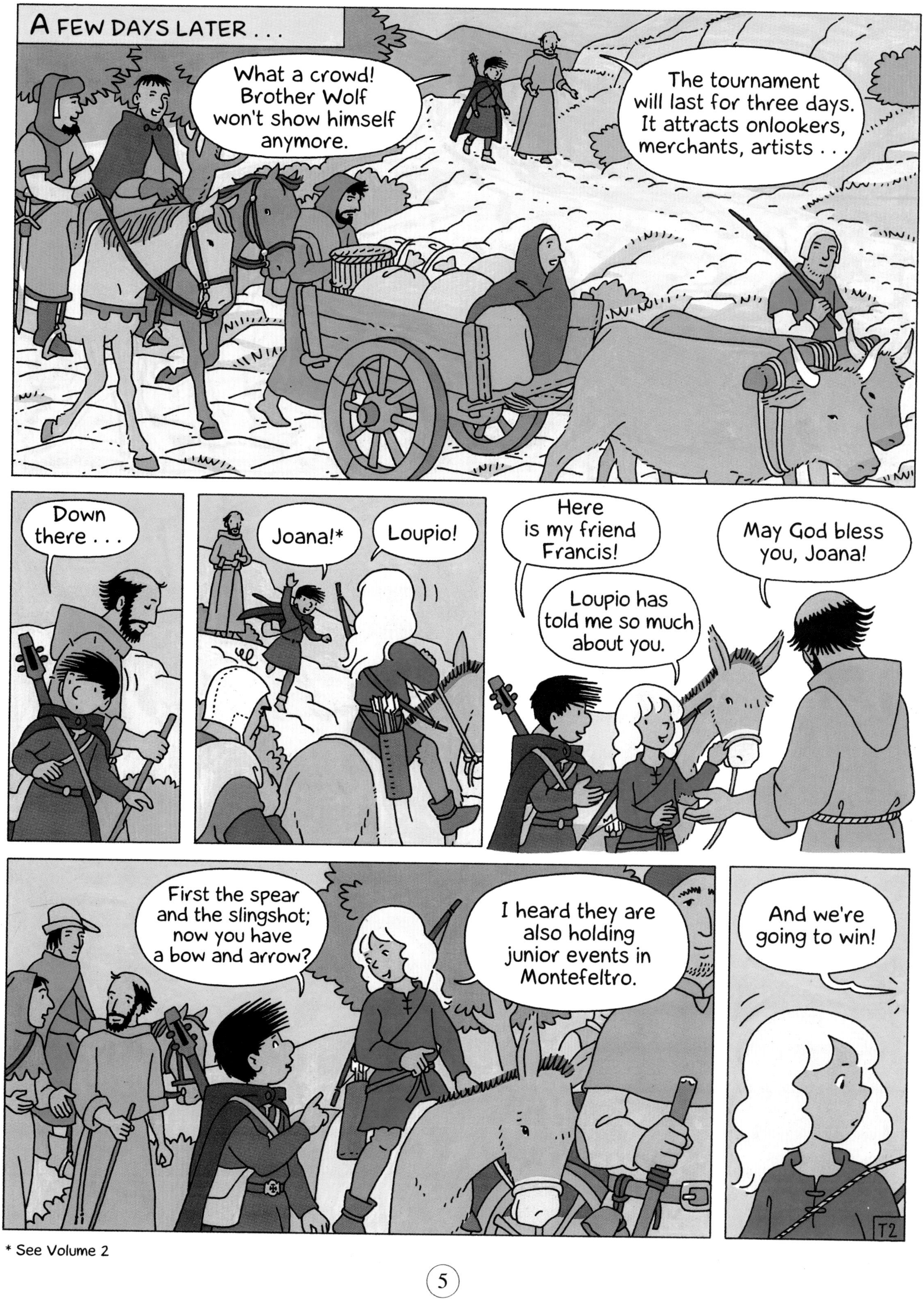
A FEW DAYS LATER . . .
What a crowd! Brother Wolf won't show himself anymore.
The tournament will last for three days. It attracts onlookers, merchants, artists . . .
Down there . . .
Joana!*
Loupio!
Here is my friend Francis!
Loupio has told me so much about you.
May God bless you, Joana!
First the spear and the slingshot; now you have a bow and arrow?
I heard they are also holding junior events in Montefeltro.
And we're going to win!
T2

* See Volume 2

Hello . . .

Who are you?

We're the pages* of the valiant knight Sir Rufus.

Do you have to be a page to compete?

No, you just need to be under fifteen.

And to be in a team of three.

A team? I didn't know that.

Don't give up! There's already the two of us.

And you're sure to find a third there.

Look at that! We're fighting midgets this year . . .

. . . and a peasant girl.

Ha ha!

Save your energy for the competition, boys!

We'll need to watch out for those three.

We'll have to find a big, strong teammate!

* In the service of a noble family, a page trained to become a squire at about fifteen, and then he trained as a knight.

SOON...

Here is Montefeltro!

What a crowd!

Ah, I see the count.

Francis! I knew you would come!

And you've brought some friends.

Joana and Loupio are interested in the Tournament of the Pages.

It will take place in the Field of the Four Winds. You'll find a place to stay there.

See you later, Francis!

Promise you'll be careful!

Come quickly, your old companions are waiting for you!

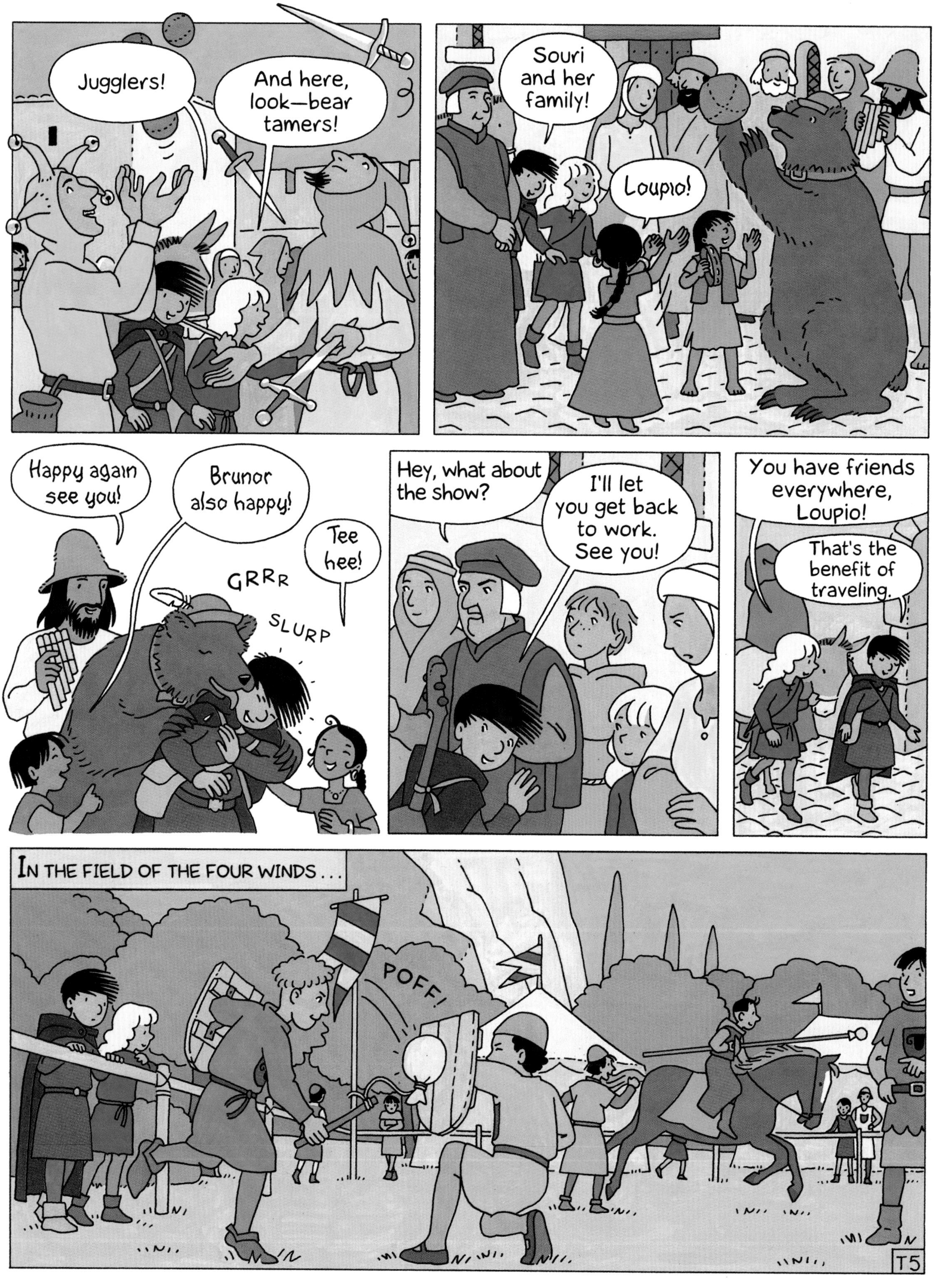
Jugglers!
And here, look—bear tamers!
Souri and her family!
Loupio!
Happy again see you!
Brunor also happy!
GRRR
SLURP
Tee hee!
Hey, what about the show?
I'll let you get back to work. See you!
You have friends everywhere, Loupio!
That's the benefit of traveling.
IN THE FIELD OF THE FOUR WINDS . . .
POFF!
T5

All these pages are already well trained.

Don't worry! Let's find our third teammate.

There's the one we need!

Team up with you two? I don't want to make a fool of myself!

Take part in the tournament? That's been my dream!

But I'm the kitchen boy in the castle and have to turn the roast over the fire all week.

Farewell, then.

No, I'm already signed up.

Hey, friend! If you dream of adventure and glory—

Keep quiet!

Oops, sorry!

TAM TARAAA

T6

Attention, all! Only those teams registered by sundown may compete in the Tournament of the Pages!

The sun's going down! Now what?

First, we register; then we keep looking.

There's only the two of you?

Uh . . . our teammate will be here soon!

What animal have you chosen for your emblem?

For our . . . ?

Um . . . ?

The wolf!

Yes, that's it!

These ladies will help you make your badges and banner.

What do you think of my wolf?

It reminds me of another one I know.

There! All set for tomorrow, my boy!

Thanks for your help!

May I keep a little thread and borrow a needle, for the third badge?

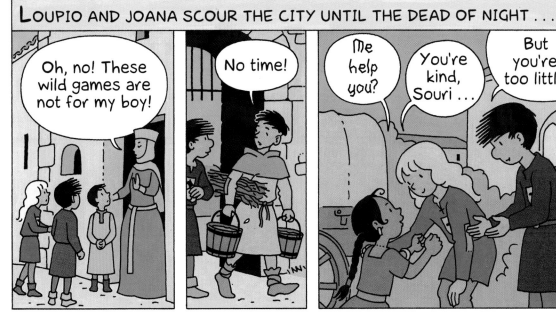

Oh, no! These wild games are not for my boy!

No time!

Me help you?

You're kind, Souri . . .

But you're too little!

AROUND MIDNIGHT . . .

The streets are deserted.

The lights are on only in the tavern . . .

. . . and the church.

What's that man doing there all alone?

He's spending the night in prayer before being armed as a knight at dawn.

Francis . . . ?

These badges—you've enrolled in the Tournament of the Pages?

Yes, but we're still missing a team member.

Entrust this worry to God and go get some sleep.

T8

11

AT DAYBREAK...

Wake up, lads! Hot soup and a tough day await you!

TAM TARAAA

Let the six teams prepare!

Now, there's really no hope.

Hey, Loupio!

Ugo?*

What miracle brings you here?

My father is in the Tournament of the Knights.

We're staying at the castle, where I met your friend Brother Francis. He said I'd find you here.

Ugo, you're our savior!

But who are you?

My name's Joana.

She and I want to be in the Tournament of the Pages. Will you join our team?

T9

*See Volumes 1 and 2

You want me? Fantastic!

Then there's not a moment to lose!

Hey!

I never would have dreamed...

Quick, the others are already in place!

Let's go, Wolves!

I remind all of you, pages and other young people, that there will be seven events in the tournament!

They will test your strength and skill...

... your bravery, fair play...

... and your musical talents ...

... all qualities of a noble knight, which some of you will be one day!

T10

13

The winning team in each event will receive three silver coins. The team that wins the most events will be named champions of the tournament and given the prize!

The first event is a match of quintain.* Choose your competitor! Let him prepare!

I've already tried that, and it hurts!

I don't know how to steer a horse.

Grisette, it's up to us to defend the honor of the Wolves!

ONE AFTER THE OTHER, THE SIX RIDERS CHARGE OFF . . .

POW!

Bravo!

Only three succeeded!

* Quintain is a lance game.

14

The second attempt!

Bravo, little brother!

POW!

You're out!

OUCH!

Hooray!

SWOOSH!

Just made it . . .

I protest!

This girl's donkey is shorter than my horse. She doesn't have to duck as much!

But he's slower!

Lend her a horse!

But, I've never . . .

WHOA!

Easy does it, Thunder!

POW!

I won!

I'm so sorry.

You were wonderful!

T12

The next event will take place at the stream.

Competitors must duel while balancing on a plank.

Ugo, now's the time to use your acrobatic skills!*

Okay. I'll give it a go.

The first duel: the Boar against the Unicorn!

Come on, little kid!

HA! BAM! AAAH!

The Wolf against the Rooster!

Go, Ugo!

Would you stand still!

AAAH!

Bravo!

SPLASH!

T13

*See Volume 2

16

AFTER LOTS OF SPLASHING . . .

In the final match, then, the Unicorn . . .

. . . and the Wolf!

BAM!

BAM!

Get up!

PLONK!

I'm the best!

SPLASH!

You put up a good fight, Ugo!

Thanks.

ATCHOO!

Quick! Join us by the fire with your friends!

T14

I ache all over!

You all are way too strong.

We don't stand a chance.

Sure you do. Don't give up, Wolves!

What's the next event?

Tug of war.

You've really got to lean back . . .

. . . dig in your heels . . .

. . . and don't give up an inch of ground!

TAM TARAAA

Take your places for the third event!

Boars to my right! Unicorns to my left!

The team that crosses the boundary of flags will be eliminated.

T15

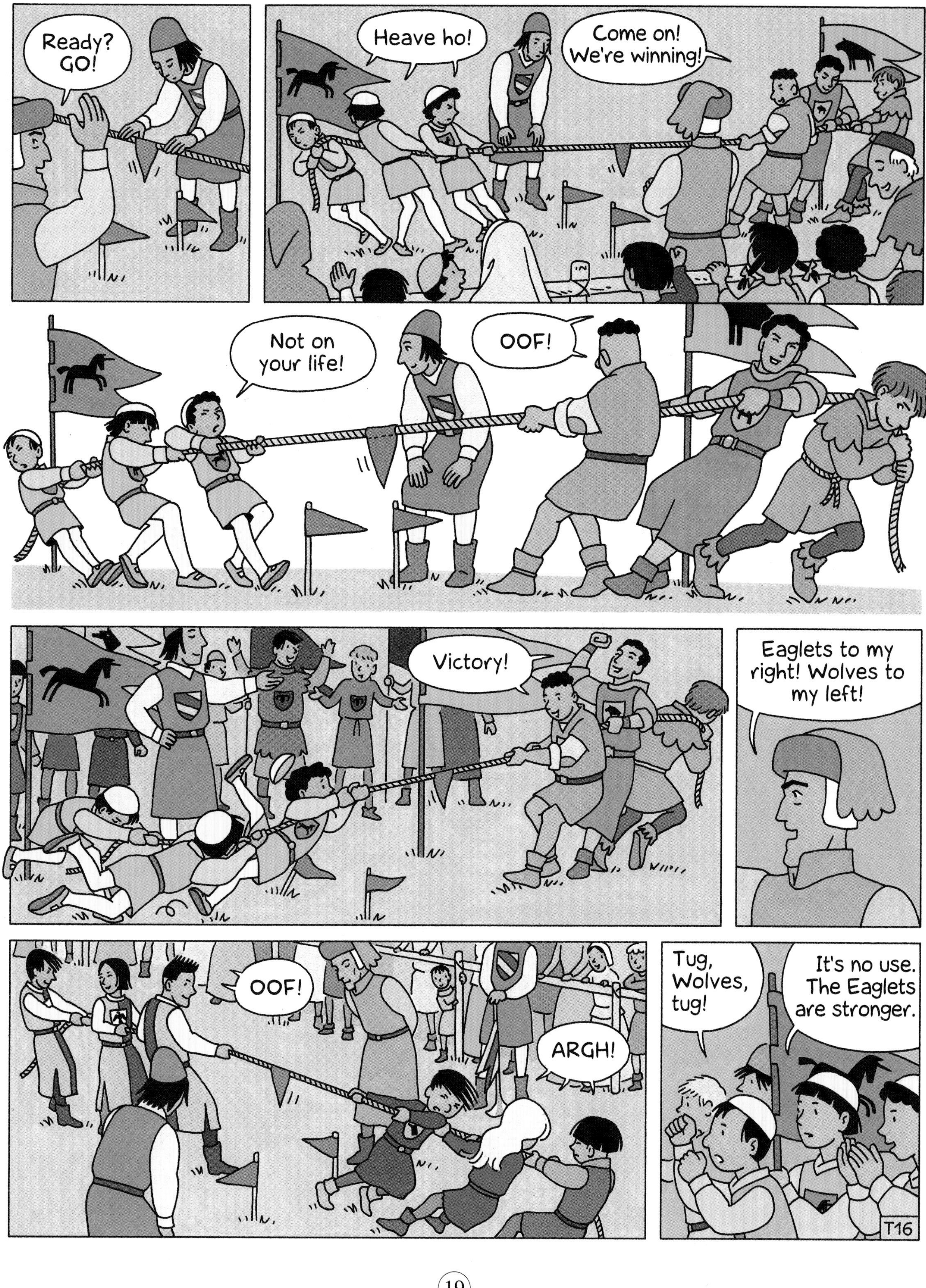
Ready? GO!
Heave ho!
Come on! We're winning!
Not on your life!
OOF!
Victory!
Eaglets to my right! Wolves to my left!
OOF!
ARGH!
Tug, Wolves, tug!
It's no use. The Eaglets are stronger.
T16

SOON...

That leaves just the Boars and the Eaglets.

The Boars will win for sure!

Time for the final round!

One moment!

Are you thirsty?

Good idea, little brother!

Hurry up! Hurry up!

Did you see that? Aldo just spilled half of that jug on the Boars' side while walking.

So what?

So, look!

Pull!

I'm ...I'm slipping!

Me, too!

Victory!

Bravo!

Oh, the cheaters!

I'm going to ...

Oh, forget it.

T17

20

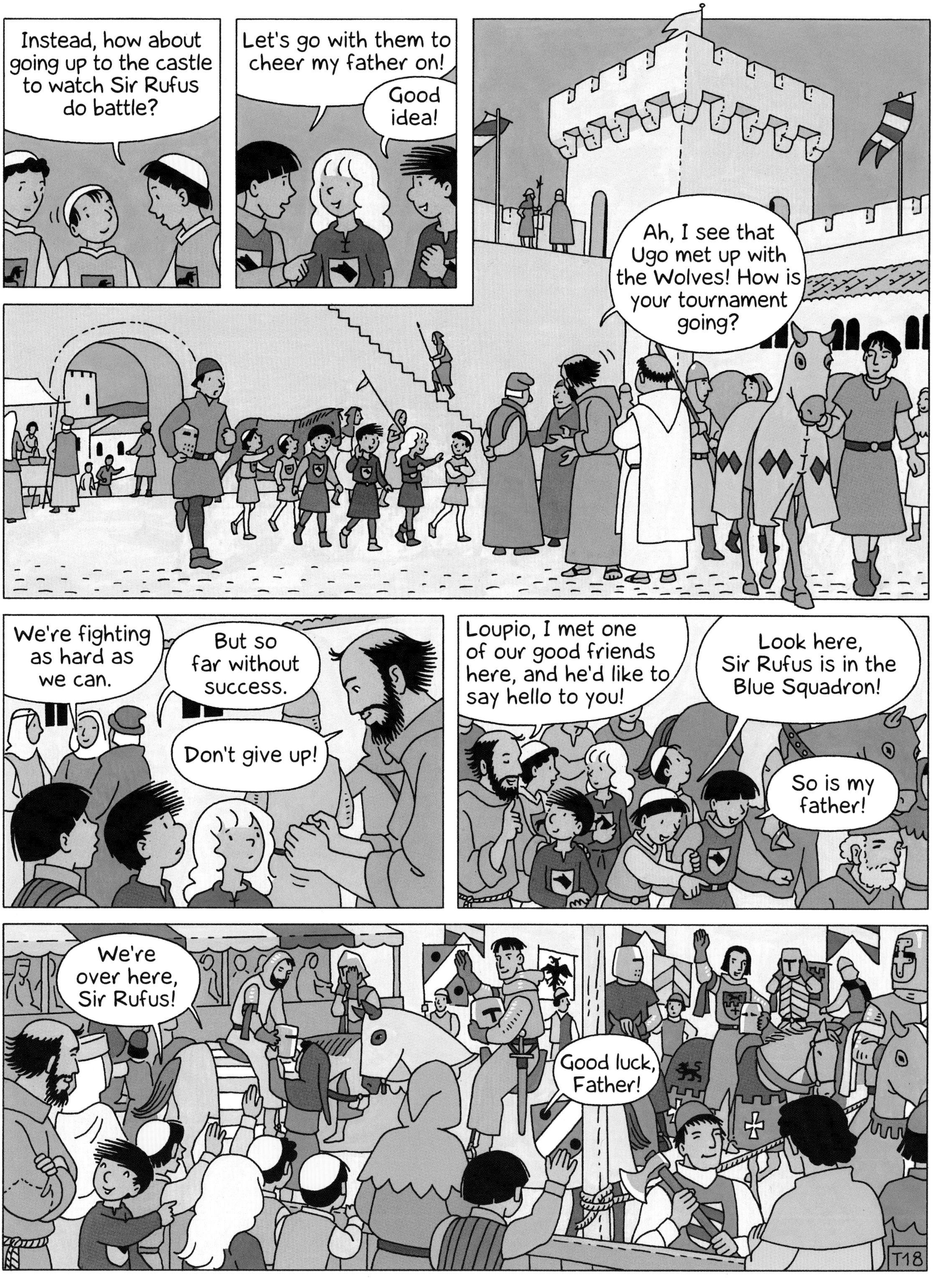
Instead, how about going up to the castle to watch Sir Rufus do battle?
Let's go with them to cheer my father on!
Good idea!
Ah, I see that Ugo met up with the Wolves! How is your tournament going?
We're fighting as hard as we can.
But so far without success.
Don't give up!
Loupio, I met one of our good friends here, and he'd like to say hello to you!
Look here, Sir Rufus is in the Blue Squadron!
So is my father!
We're over here, Sir Rufus!
Good luck, Father!
T18

As soon as the rope is cut, they'll charge toward the Yellows and try to take their scarves.

CLACK!

What a free-for-all!

Rufus has already eliminated two Yellows!

Oh, no! Father has fallen!

Three Yellows are attacking him!

Look! One of his teammates is coming to the rescue!

T19

22

LATER...

Whew, the match is over.

Father, I was so afraid for you!

This knight got me out of a tight spot.

Hello, Loupio!

He knows my name?

Orlando!*

So, you've taken up arms again?

Only for the tournament.

Our hospice is sorely in need of money, so I've come to try my luck!

LATER...

Did you see Rufus take a scarf with one stroke of the sword? SWISH!

And my father, one against three? WHOOSH!

Tomorrow, we'll have to be just as brave!

* See Volume 1

AFTER A RESTFUL NIGHT...

What's on the program today?

First, archery. Joana is already warming up.

Then, swordplay. And finally, something for you—the test of agility.

If it doesn't involve getting hit, I volunteer!

Then I'll take the swordplay.

FINALLY, THAT MORNING, FATE SMILES ON THE WOLVES...

CHOCK

She's a remarkable archer!

How do you do it?

Oh, I just aim.

That's what I do, too.

But I train a lot while I'm tending my sheep.

Just one more match for victory. The Rooster versus the Wolf!

CHOCK

Nice shot!

Go on. Show me how it's done!

24

OOH!

Bull's-eye!

I've . . . I've . . .

You've won!

We are the champions! We are the champions!

Come, come, my boy! The singing contest isn't until tomorrow.

TAM TARAAA

Take your places for the fifth event!

The first to cut down his dummy is the winner. Ready?

GO!

WHACK!

WHACK! WHACK!

CRACK!

PLINK!

This sword is . . . so . . . heavy.

Hit it, Loupio!

YEE-HAAA!

WHACK!

ARRGH!

Oops!

HA HA HA! HO HO

Victory!

I was lousy.

Ooh, my arm!

You don't stand a chance against Maximo.

TAM TARAAA

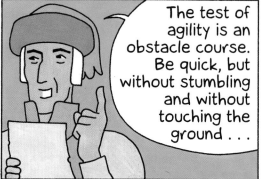

The test of agility is an obstacle course. Be quick, but without stumbling and without touching the ground . . .

THE ROOSTER SETS OFF FIRST . . .

Go!

T23

THEN THE BOAR...
WHOA!

THE EAGLET...

THE RAM...
WHOOPS!

THE UNICORN...

AND FINALLY...
Go on, Ugo!

What ease!
What speed!

DING!

The Wolf was the fastest!

Bravo!
Hooray, Wolves!
Woo-hoo!

Two victories for the Wolves. What a good day!

Whoohoo! If you win the musical contest tomorrow, Loupio, we win the tournament!

Not so fast! The Eaglets have also won two events.

And I heard Mona singing. She's very gifted!

LATER...
I can practice here, where it's quiet.

T24

♪ ♫ So brave and true, this troubadour crew! They call us the wolves! ♪ ♫

How lovely, Loupio!

Mona?

Were you looking for peace and quiet too?

No, I'm going to see a friend.

A famous composer who lives not far from here.

Oh, really?

He knows hundreds of songs and owns an amazing collection of old and beautiful instruments . . .

And he lives nearby?

Very near. Want to come?

He'd love to meet you.

Likewise!

Your friend lives in a mill?

Yes, he likes the music of the water going around the wheel.

What a poet he must be!

After you.

T25

28

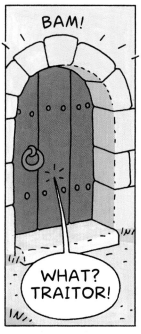

BAM!

WHAT? TRAITOR!

My lute! My cloak!

Take away his tunic and shoes as well!

Don't hurt him, okay? I don't want any trouble!

Don't worry, miller! Our friend Loupio is just going to have a little rest.

Just put him in here, the door is very solid.

Give me back my lute and my clothes!

You'll get everything back! But first, another Loupio needs them . . .

. . . one who, alas, doesn't sing as well.

CHEATERS! SCOUNDRELS!

You can yell all you like. With the noise of the mill, no one will hear you.

For his room and board.

Let him free tomorrow evening.

By then we'll have won the tournament and been long gone.

T26

29

Come on, miller! I'm hungry!

I'm coming, I'm coming . . .

I'm cold, too!

Put on one of those sacks.

Where's Loupio?

Your friend? I saw him at the castle.

Well, I'm going to bed.

It's almost dawn. What am I going to do?

WHOOOO

Brother Wolf! I knew you'd come!

Run! Go and warn my friends!

Zzzz . . .

Sniff Sniff

Brrr . . .

My blanket!

Brother Wolf?

Joana, something's happened to Loupio!

Hmm?

T 27

The path ends here.

TAP TAP

What do you want?

We're looking for our friend, with a red cloak and . . .

I haven't seen anything.

GRRR

Help!

BAM! BAM!

I'm here, my friends!

GRRR

Where's the key?

I'm not saying anything!

Watch him. I'll run for help!

Hold back your animal, boy. I'll give you the key.

Don't move!

Grrrr

T28

31

We thank the Countess of Montefeltro for honoring us with her presence at this final event in the Tournament of the Pages.

And we begin, of course, with the song of the Rooster!

Tee hee!

♪ There ♫ once was a shepheeeerd

Hmm . . .

Thank you.

The Eaglets' candidate!

♫ The ♪ lovely little bird no more do I hear. It has flown away; it has disappeared. ♫ ♫

Now that's what I call singing.

Well done, young maiden!

IN THE MEANTIME . . .

I have something better than a key!

Huh? What . . .

Open door, Brunor!

Noooo!

CRACK!

Thank you, everyone!

T29

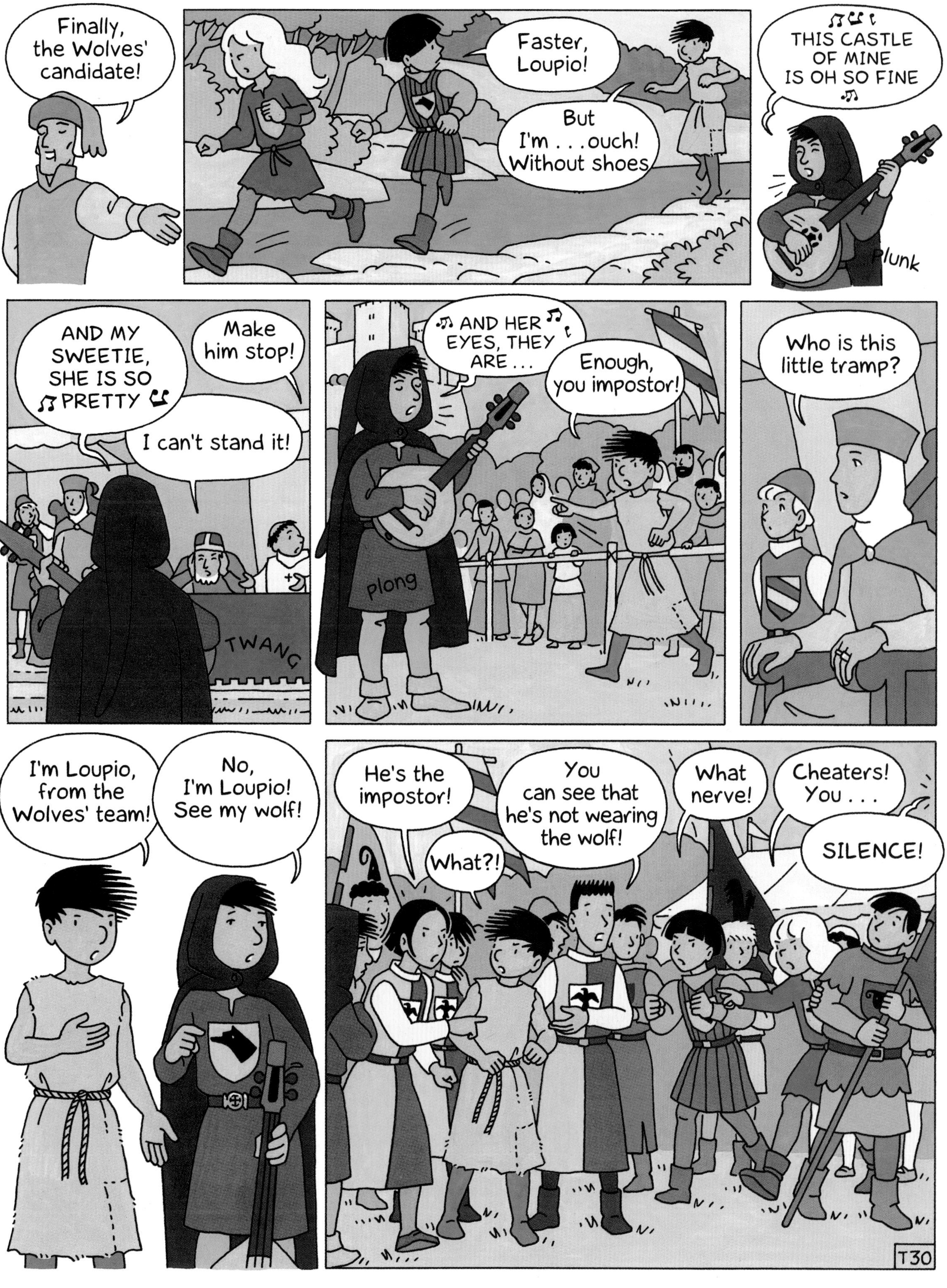
Finally, the Wolves' candidate!
Faster, Loupio!
But I'm . . . ouch! Without shoes
THIS CASTLE OF MINE IS OH SO FINE
Plunk
AND MY SWEETIE, SHE IS SO PRETTY
Make him stop!
I can't stand it!
TWANG
AND HER EYES, THEY ARE . . .
Enough, you impostor!
plong
Who is this little tramp?
I'm Loupio, from the Wolves' team!
No, I'm Loupio! See my wolf!
He's the impostor!
What?!
You can see that he's not wearing the wolf!
What nerve!
Cheaters! You . . .
SILENCE!
T30

Enough of this! Show us your wolf and we'll listen to you.

Oooh!

Ooh!

How very unusual . . .

But then who's the other one?

A prankster, gentlemen!

Give it to me! Your prank was funny, but it has gone on far too long!

Sing, Loupio!

♪ ♫ ♪
So brave and true, this troubadour crew! They call us the wolves! By day, by night, we're ready to fight! Watch out for the wolves!
♪ ♫ ♪

Bravo!

Thank you! The jury will now decide.

TAM TARAAA

In the singing competition, victory goes to the Wolves, whom I also declare as champions of the Tournament of the Pages!

Hooray!

Long live the Wolves!

The prizes will be awarded at the end of the Tournament of the Knights!

Come on, don't be sad.

Did you really want to win that much?

Oh, no! It's just that tomorrow we'll have to say farewell.

You'll see—our paths will cross again.

Loupio, we . . .

Well, well, it's your friend the miller.

Hey you! My door is broken. Someone must pay for it.

What are you talking about?

Must I speak to your father about it?

Uh . . . that's okay! Wait for us after the award ceremony.

You're going to tell on us, aren't you?

Let's forget it. After all, the night at the mill gave me time to finish my song!

35

THAT AFTERNOON, IN THE CASTLE COURTYARD...

This year, no one could beat Rufus!

And Vittorio earned second place!

Shh! There's a third prize—

Finally, I am pleased to award this prize money to our dear Orlando of Cortone!

Bravo!

Hooray!

And now, noble sires and ladies, let us hail the valiant winners of the Tournament of the Pages!

To the Unicorns, three silver coins.

To the Rams, three silver coins.

To the Eaglets, six silver coins.

T33

36

To the Wolves, champions of the tournament, nine silver coins and a special prize.

This splendid piglet, ready for roasting!

HO HO! HA HA!

Oink!

LATER...

Loupio, you look disappointed.

I expected more... a sword, a harp...

What are we supposed to do with that animal?

Give it to Orlando for his hospice!

Oh, yes. Why not even deliver it to him in person?

Good idea, Loupio! If my father gives me permission, I'll go with you!

A long trip with you two?! Now, that's the kind of prize I like!

NEVER HAD THE ROADS OF ITALY SEEN SUCH A TROOP...

So brave and true, this troubadour crew! They call us the wolves!

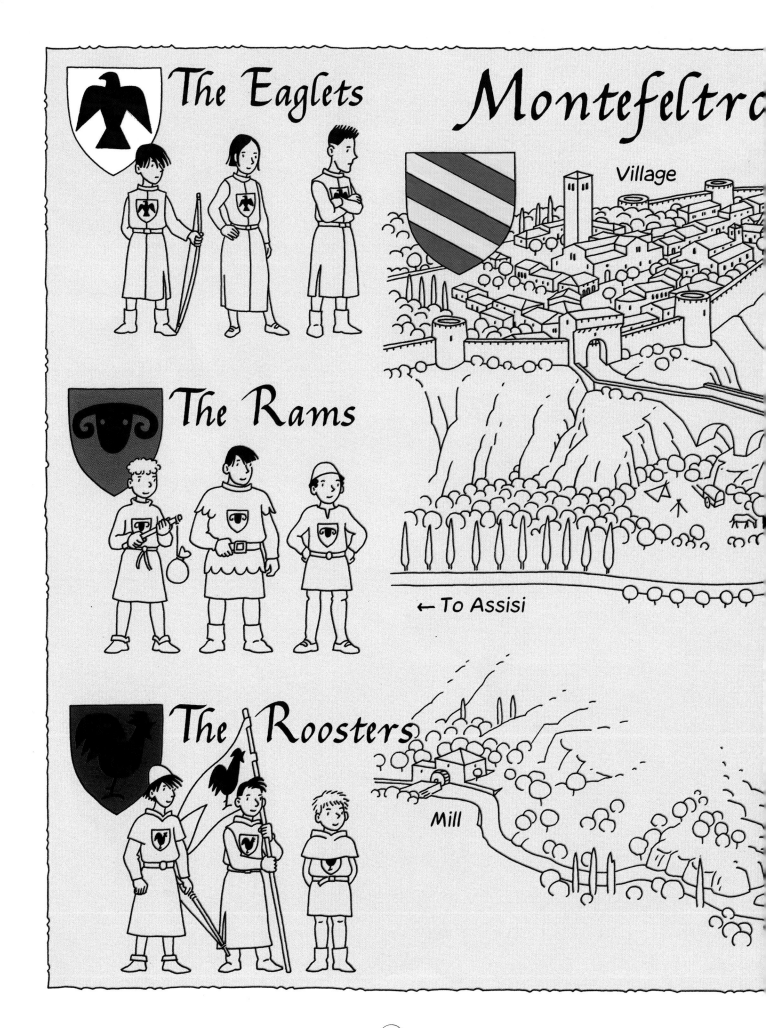

The Eaglets

Montefeltro

Village

The Rams

← To Assisi

The Roosters

Mill

Castle

The Unicorns

The Wolves

Field of
the Four Winds

The Boars

Stream

39

We Are the Wolves

REFRAIN

So brave and true, this trou-ba-dour crew! They call us the Wolves! By

day, by night, we're rea - dy to fight! Watch out for the Wolves!

VERSES

Our life is so grand to-ge-ther as friends with des-tin-ies tied. Both

good luck and bad luck our friend-ship trans-cends; we're Wolves side by side.

Refrain: So brave and true, this troubadour crew! They call us the Wolves!
By day, by night, we're ready to fight! Watch out for the Wolves!

Verses:

Our life is so grand
together as friends
with destinies tied.
Both good luck and bad luck
our friendship transcends;
We're Wolves side by side.

Our skills are outmatched,
more often than not.
But we stand and fight!
We circle the wolf pack
while enemies plot.
Like Wolves, we unite!

When victory is won
and battles have ceased,
we'll sing out our tune.
With food, fun and fanfare,
we'll gather to feast.
We'll howl at the moon.

Although he competes,
and plays as to win,
a wolf never gloats.
Our hearts aren't conceited
or hardened with sin,
but soft as Wolves' coats.

Original French verses by Jean-François Kieffer - Set to a Renaissance melody